My Voice is Silent to My Fears

(Selected Poems and Writings)

By Peter Stavropoulos

Contents:

In the beginning was the Word

And the Word was Good

And all Spoke the Word

And the Word was Love

And all Loved the Word.

In the beginning was the Word

And the Word became Days

And Days to Life

And Life to Poetry.

Let us begin here

With a sentence

And the sentence is

Love

Let us begin here

With a word

And the word is

Forever

Let us begin here

With a taste of certainty

And the certainty is

You

I Thought about you

And lost my memory

In time

I could not remember

The loss

And yet

In you

I have a memory

Of a happier time

In beauty there is myth

I am the brave hero

In Love there is legend

I am the blind storyteller

In truth there is fiction

I am the vagabond poet

In honour there is glory

I am the hopeless romantic

The education of the young mind

The education of the young mind

Took place

Behind closed doors

Because that mind –

Initially free –

Had to be

Taught –

The value of freedom.

The education of the young mind

Took place

In an open space

Because that mind –

Once closed –

Had to be

Set free

To explore itself.

The poet and the rock

The rock said

I am a rock

The poet said

I know

The poet and the rock

The rock said

I am a poet

The poet said

I am a rock

By some miracle

I believe in You

The miracle

Of You

By some stroke

Of luck

I found You

To believe in

The challenge

Is to begin at

The beginning.

The challenge

Is to determine

What that is.

And start again.

The Witch Doctor's Son

He was the first African to do medicine at Oxford. "A bright fellow quite brilliant for a black man" – how he hated those words. He had been top in his class and tomorrow were his final exams. In his room that night he prepared the spell to ensure his success.

The Undertaker's Widow

At the funeral she presented a composed face to the world. "At least his coffin is the finest," she thought. At home she knew that, with his death, the business could no longer compete and she began to work on another fine coffin. "Such is life and work," she thought.

In Escalated Silence

In escalated silence

I sing to you

Words that have no meaning

Except in silence

Words that pretend, pervade meaning

But have none in reality

Words that exchange thoughts

And such their power

And this I say to you

Without a sound.

If I say

Doesn't it change

The course we've taken

If I say

I Love you?

Doesn't it mean

The end of what we had

If what we had

Was a beginning?

The Lord in a simple way

The Lord in a simple way

Gave me you

He did

To forgive me

 And I have promised you

 My Love

<u>A Poet's Pleasure</u>

My mind thinks.

My heart knows.

Together, the hand writes, pleasing both.

15

I move

To be with you

You are my motion

And my speech

I learn

By teaching you

Words I cannot

Speak

Wish upon

Wish upon

Another's heart

Let her be happy

Let her be strong

Let her Love right the wrong

Wish upon

Another's mind

Let it seek

Let it be free

Let its knowledge find me

Wish upon

Another's soul

Let us journey

Let us travel far

Let our Love guide the star

Beauty lies

Within your eyes

I can't speak

Of what I seek

Its mystery

A majesty

No purpose seems

To fit dreams

Beneath the lid

Your eyes hid

18

Without possibility

I exist

To be any less

Would imply

A beginning

And an end

I would be

Sure

Of that

The art of writing

To one you know

Of the Love you know

Is the art

Of making false

Everything that isn't

Loneliness

I could not find loneliness

Because it searched for me

Its thoughts were of happiness

Brought by misery

I could not escape loneliness

Because it found in me

A home of such kindness

It alone could be

Empty Without You

Emptiness means little without you

Words alone cannot equal two

You meant little to me before we met

The world alone closed every sunset

I had fought and lost again

What thought had found to gain

Its memory a frozen ocean

Without you Love's empty notion

My face is not the face you know

It belongs to me

My face is not the only thing I share

I share myself

And the one I Love

In the everlasting fragrance

Of the sound

Of your love

I bathe and notice

Each winding minute

To your door

To your door

The key to which

Unlocks each and every

Passage in my heart

Chances

Each chance

A new belief

Something new

A heart's relief

Each romance

A lover's hue

Finding Love

Each in you

The truth is

The truth is

As it has always been

Unchanging

Undeniable

Unswerving

Unspoken

The giver

And the receiver

The one and the only.

Dear Lord

I will find

A way

There is no doubt

No doubt

In me

No doubt

In You

No doubt

In the way

To begin with

I know very little
Of honour.

I receive
A gift
With your presence.

And acknowledge
My life
As worthless.

I do not pretend
The years

Pass gracefully.

I do not have a claim
On permanence.

I know what I value.

I know that before me
Have lived many great individuals –
All dust now.

To join them
As dust
Is an honour.

<u>In the Time of the Greeks</u>

"It is a paradox

That these fields should be covered in flowers and it be spring.

What an irony

That I'm not dead

A pleasing irony, yes, a pleasing irony."

With this he laughed and the fields echoed with his laughter.

Two days earlier

This had been the scene of a bitter battle

Between the warring states of

Athens and Sparta.

A battle that had raged for many hours

When finally it moved on.

On the first day after battle the countryside was wild with cries, now only his lone laughter heralded day two.

These fields lay close to the city of Hermos,

In the Peloponnesus,

A city that had been able to remain neutral in the war.

Luckily the battle had avoided the city,

And on this day life was returning to normal.

A girl from the city,

Ethene by name,

Decided, as the day was fine,

To spend some time in these fields.

A rich assortment of flowers was to be found where the man lay dying,

And unknowingly she went there.

Her first sight of him was devastating
As his flesh turned to meet her.

He too was shocked.

She stood motionless as she tried to understand the sight she beheld.

"Quiet, do not be scared
I am beyond harming you
And beyond care."

"I do not understand.
What is this?

Do you speak?"

"I speak to comfort you

Although there is little comfort here."

"Are you human?

Do you breathe?"

"I breathe, my girl.

As do you."

"Oh God!

This cannot be true.

Poor man, poor, poor man. How can I help you?"

"God cannot help me, neither you,

Although you both may try,

I do not wish it."

With this she started to cry.

"Do not cry

Cannot you see that I am content?

Come sit near me awhile."

"I can't bear it

And shan't."

Terrified and confused

She ran off,

Leaving him there alone

Although not as she had found him.

The rest of the day and night

Her thoughts were with him

And her secretive silence was, to her,

Another surprise.

Next day she found him still alive.

"Yes, my girl,

I still live.

And how are you?"

"I wish to help you,

And if you must die

I do not know how."

"As I told you yesterday,

Sit with me.

This day is equally as fine."

"The day is fine

But how can you care for it?"

"I care for it

Because I am free

And without care.

The day breathes for me

And speaks."

"I see you are mad

And I am mad to listen to you.

I will go to get help

Perhaps it is not too late."

"Yes I am mad

But do not go

I have very little time left.

Can you not see I am beyond help?"

She stood silent

At the undeniable truth

Of this statement

And after a while sat near him.

"What is your name?"

"I am Ethene, daughter of Thermistocles,

From the city of Hermos."

"And your age?"

"Eighteen this summer."

"I am Aristophes, son of Domocles,

From the mighty city of Athens.

Dead at twenty six."

"Cannot I do something for you?

Perhaps a drink?"

"Yes, perhaps a drink."

She handed him her water container

But he,

Unable to help himself,

Was helped by her.

"I am very pleased to have met you, Ethene."

She did not know how to answer this.

"Cannot I do something for you?"

"Sir, do not joke,

Please."

"I do not joke

And I would not joke with you."

For the first time in days he fought the desire to live.

"Tell me a little about yourself, Ethene."

"There is nothing much to tell

And nothing of worth to tell now."

"Am I not the best judge

Of what is worthy now?

Shall we talk of politics

Or war or practicalities?"

"I am a simple farm girl

Born near Hermos, on my parents farm.

I have been raised in obedience to the

Teachings of the Gods and spend my days

With my family in common love.

Nature is my play fellow but she gives me no

Friendship now."

"Why the misery?

Do not let my circumstances sadden you.

Have I not told you it is as I wish

And I will not have you saddened."

"Yes I have heard

But I cannot understand this wish.

Is life not better than death?

Even life as a cripple?"

"It is not death I seek

Nor life that I scorn

As with all men

Happiness is my one wish."

"Cannot you find happiness in life?"

"It has failed me.

Or I failed it?

No matter, life will soon not be a question."

"I am so sorry!"

"I do not wish to change your sorrow.

Sit beside me still

Your beauty leaves room for no other pain."

They sat there quietly for a while,

A strange scene.

"You give a strange flattery."

"You deserve better."

"What manner of man

Is it

That I speak to?"

"A normal man?"

"No, no normal man."

"A soldier of Athens

Downed in battle."

"Yes, and more."

"A soldier of Athens

Downed in battle

Sharing his final hours

With a beautiful maiden."

"Yes, and more still, I'm sure."

"Yes more

As every man is more than meets the eye."

"You speak as a philosopher."

"I am

As is every soldier."

"You speak proudly of that."

"I do

As do all philosophers."

"You jest again

This time in riddles."

"I am sorry.

You are my guest."

"Your guest!?"

"You are welcome here."

"Then please

Tell me something of yourself,

I would like to know.

And if there is someone

You would like a message sent to

Then I can help you."

"The people I care about

Will know of my fate

By my absence.

Thank you for your offer."

"Will you not tell me

How you came to be here?"

"I am a volunteer

In the Athenian army

And a proud fighter

Who has met his fate."

"All men's fate is this

Why do you make more of it

And less of it

In this manner?"

"Because for me

It has arrived welcomed

And not too soon."

"You do not strike me

As a melancholic."

"And yet I am."

"Are you?"

"Do not I welcome death?"

"Perhaps you are resigned to your fate.

Or rather death than life as a cripple."

"I rather death than any life.

There I have said it plainly.

And to whom have I said it?

A girl so full of life and unmarked

By tragedy as I have ever seen.

And when do I say it?

In my last hours

Prior to inflicting upon her, my death.

I am beyond contempt

Leave me now."

"Do you think I have not felt

The pain of tragedy?"

"I hope not,

I think not yet."

"And do you think

Only you have?"

"Not only I

But I yes."

"Shall I go then and leave

Unmarked?"

"Yes go."

"And if I go
Will you think of me
As you have thought?"

"I will not blame you."

"Would you leave
A dying man?"

"No.
But you are not I."

"I know, you have felt tragedy."

"Do not mock me."

"I am sorry if I sounded
Cruel."

"It is forgotten
Now please leave."

"Now you want me to leave.
It seems only you
Can feel for others.
I will not go!"

"Do not be spiteful,
Or rebellious,
Go.
I will not think the less of you

Because of it."

"That is generous of you."

"Not generous."

"I will stay and comfort you

Until the end.

And if it is true

That only those who have suffered

At the hands of life

Can feel for others

Then I must stay and care for you

To prove you wrong

Or to prove you right."

"Now who is the philosopher?"

"You, the soldier."

They smiled and laughed together,

Happily,

Forgetting where they were.

Then came a time that passed

Without any words.

"Is it chance

That brought you here,

Ethene?"

"Yes chance, and the trees

And the flowers."

"Yes the flowers

Are beautiful

I have thought of them also."

He paused,

Regretting these words.

"And what else has brought you here?"

"That is in itself enough

But I also wished

To leave the farm and the city

And be by myself."

"And why was that?"

"For the peace."

"The peace!"

"Yes, the peace
And the quiet.
Somewhere, where I could be alone
With my thoughts."

"Yes I understand.
And then I came along
To disrupt all that
And put you into this nightmare.
Please leave, I cannot bear to have
This inflicted upon you."

"I wish to stay.
It is my choice."

"But why?

Do not be stubborn.

Forget our little argument before."

"I am not being stubborn.

I want to stay

Because I know I belong here."

"You belong here?"

"Yes, do not ask me why.

I do not know why.

But I know I belong here.

I am comfortable here."

"Comfortable, with a dying man

Next to you?"

"It is a mystery to me also.

But I do not want to leave."

"You have given the meaning of compassion

New heights."

"It is not compassion

Or selflessness.

I belong here.

And if I leave

All the glory

And all the happiness

Of the world cannot

Replace this.

And it seems the more I speak

The more I know."

"Then speak more."

"From childhood to now

My family and I

Have lived happy lives.

We have given each other

Everything of ourselves.

You could not wish to see

A happier family.

This is not to say

That we have not had

Some tragedy in our lives.

We have.

We've had death and disease

And the fury of nature's whims

And poverty.

And now in the midst of poverty,

Threatened by war.

But this was all not our doing

And within this we lived,

Or tried to live, happily

And as best we could

According to the laws of the Gods.

The other people of the city,

Or at least the majority, were like us

And each tried to live as was correct.

This is as much as I can explain,

If you can call it an explanation,

And I belong here."

It began to drizzle then

And then to shower

And just when he began to worry for her,

t stopped.

"Promise me one thing, Ethene."

"And what is that?
You know I will not leave."

"Promise me you will never do as I have done.
Never submit to death."

"Don't be silly."

"I am not being silly.
Promise, and swear to a dying man
This promise."

"I swear."

How the day had developed

And how she came to be there

Seemed like a dream to her.

<u>Thicker Than Blood</u>

<u>Part One:</u>

His weight rested easily in the chair. The big man, although appearing awkward, sat relaxed comforted by the early morning winter sun. From the yard, beyond the fence, he could see the business of the street and hear, if he wished, the cars or hurrying footsteps.

*

Often he ventured from the yard, "for exercise" he would say. And when I looked I would find him beyond what I thought his crippled brain would permit. I ask him sometimes where he has been and his reply is always vague "around the block." People tell me that when they meet him he seems happy and his conversation is bright. When I ask him about these meetings he doesn't remember.

*

"How are you, Papa?"

"Better ….. everyday better. I don't say I get perfect but I improve. When I get sick, when I get sss….."

"Stroke."

"Stroke. When I get stroke doctors say throw away, no good any more. But now I am better. I don't say perfect but not for throw away. You, are you good?"

"Yes good, Papa, good."

*

Half blinded as he is, he spends most of his time in the yard, if the Sun is out, or bothering my mother with his well meaning humour. His walks have extended the limits of his exile but they too are marked by the inevitability of his return.

*

"How are you today, Papa?"

"Better ….. everyday better. I don't say I –"

"Tell me, what are you doing today?"

"Nothing, I walk, sit here. I walk all day, never stop. See, I have sweat on my head from my walk this morning. When I get better I do more. What doctors say, I get better?"

"Yes, slowly, everyday you get better. But you must do more, walk, exercise, work around the house, help Mama more."

"Yes, but my eyes, that is the problem. I not see perfect. If I see-"

"Will you listen to the football today, Papa? Today is the Grand Final between Carlton and Richmond."

"Football! Killer game. What Collingwood do, lose?"

"Collingwood do very bad this year, almost last, a lot of trouble at the club. Collingwood is a very bad team, always trouble, never win premiership. You should change to Hawthorn like Maria and me."

"No, I always Collingwood. Someday, they win, no matter, I stay Collingwood."

"Collingwood a bad team."

"I stay Collingwood."

"All right, as you wish, You're very loyal, Papa."

"Hawthorn lose?"

"Yes, Hawthorn lose to Carlton in Semi-Final."

"You change to Carlton? Hawthorn always lose."

"All right, we see next year."

Having scored a point in our little verbal joust 'the old man' sits relaxed and throws a smile at me, 'the scorer'.

*

"And you, what you do today?"

"Today I see Adele and if the weather remains fine we'll go for a picnic and maybe tonight we'll go to a dance."

"What day today?"

"Saturday."

"Good, enjoy yourself. You are young, enjoy!"

"Did you enjoy yourself when you where young? Did you go dancing? Hey, did you practice what you preach?"

Spotting my mother from the corner of his eye and containing the smile he has reserved for her, he continues.

"Yes we dance to morning. But now Mama has no energy, too old."

My mother, immune, makes no reply.

"Was it good in Greece when you were young?"

"Yes, before war, very good."

"Better than Australia?"

"I don't say better, I am Greek. Greece before the war was good but after very bad. Poor, very poor, no food, trouble everywhere. Australia good country."

With mention of 'the war' I try to relate the soldier so often described to me with 'the old man'. The attempt brings an unwelcomed respect of war.

*

From within the house I hear a faint familiar tune heralding the start of the Greek half hour on radio. I could, if I wish, keep my father here longer with often asked questions about Greece and Australia. I could ask him to describe Greece to me or his village or his early days here. Instead, I let him know the show has started and watch him leave in a tell-tale hurry.

Part Two:

"Good morning Papa, are you well?"

"Yes good, and you?"

"Good. Are you ready to visit the doctor, Papa?"

"I not know. Sophia, I got everything?"

"Yes, everything in your pockets. But you shave again, you leave half your face with whiskers."

"No. I shave all right."

"Paul, is his face clean?"

"No, you've missed half your whiskers, Papa. Come on, I'll shave you."

I give 'the old man' a shave and after a few readying good byes, head off for our appointment.

The drive to the hospital is quiet, when I offer a topic for conversation he tries but is disinterested.

"Don't worry about the doctor, Papa. We're only going to check that your eye infection has cleared up. It's all right."

"I no worry."

"I'm glad you're not worried, Papa."

He remains quiet and we reach the hospital without another word.

*

Hand in hand we enter the reception area and make our way to the only queue in the room.

When it is our turn, "Hello, my father has an appointment to see the doctor today."

"Hello," the receptionist replies and smiles. "Can I see your appointment card, please?"

I hand it to her as smoothly as possible.

"Can I have your father's name, please?"

"Vasilios Papadopoulos."

"How do you spell that, please?"

"P – A – P – A – D – O – P – O – U – L – O – S"

"And your address, please?"

"Sixty Six, Rathmines Street, Fairfield."

"Here you are."

She hands me back the appointment card with my father's name now typed on and two other slips of paper. One bearing adhesive labels with my father's name and patient number in bold type.

"Take the lift, doctor's rooms are on the first floor on your right," she says pointing to the lifts.

"Thank you," I reply.

"Thank you," the receptionist says, smiling.

*

Making our way to the lift we avoid most obstacles. Only a fast moving orderly gives us any cause for concern. As per instructions we arrive at the doctor's reception on the first floor.

"Hello, I was told to come here, um, my father has an appointment to see the doctor."

"May I see you're appointment form, please?"

I leave all our forms in this receptionist's capable hands. She peels off one of the labels and duly registers 'the old man.'

"Here you are," She says, returning the forms to me.

"Please take a seat."

"Thank you."

She was also very helpful, I think.

I look around and am relieved to see that there is only one other person waiting to see the doctor. We make ourselves comfortable on the bench and wait.

"We see doctor now?"

"In a little while, Papa."

"How my eye look?"

"Good, your infection has almost gone, this time next week it should be completely cleared," and, I add reassuringly, "I think the doctor will quickly see that the nfection has gone and send us on our way. No need to worry, Papa."

"I no worry."

"Is there something you want, Papa? A drink?"

"Is there a toilet near?"

I should have known. At reception I ask if there is a toilet nearby.

"Yes, by the lifts on the left."

She is indeed helpful.

On our return I see that the person, who was waiting with us, has gone in to see the doctor. I search through a pile of magazines and find an interesting Women's Weekly. I begin to read an article 'one patient seeing the doctor for a check up' long when – Papadopoulos! – shouts a smiling face.

*

My father turns and presents himself to the man shouting his name.

"Papadopoulos!"

Beside my father stands a hospital cleaner, broom in hand.

"Papadopoulos! How are you? Many years since I see you."

The man is easily recognisable to me as Greek. He becomes subdued when he receives a questioning stare in reply.

"Papadopoulos, my friend, how are you?"

I explain, "His eyesight is very bad. He suffered a stroke a couple of years ago."

"Oh ..... I see," he replies.

Taken aback by the stranger now in front of him, he is now speechless.

'The old man' interjects, "Sorry, I am sick, I get sss ...."

"Stroke, Papa."

"Stroke. I no see perfect. Do I know you?"

"Vasily, it's Christos Yanapoulos! We had shops together in South Yarra, in Sixty Five."

He tries again.

"Christos Yanapoulos from Kalamata."

These words have that blend of an introduction and re-living old memories, with which I am now familiar.

"Christos Yanapoulos. Christos, friend, how are you?"

Recognition and smiles all around. Warm handshakes are exchanged.

"Good, and how are you, friend?"

"Good. Sorry I no see you. I have sss....."

"Stroke," I answer before the question is asked.

"Stroke. I have Stroke. I no see perfect."

"What happened, friend?" Enquires a concerned Christos.

'The old man', again, "Blood press, worry, too much worry."

I elaborate, "He worked too hard. Two, sometimes three jobs. Plus he worried too much about many things. He always tried to do too many things."

"I was stupid," adds my father, matter of factly.

"Two years ago he had a stroke which affected parts of his brain." I place a cupped hand over the back of my head.

"The stroke affected his right side, he lost strength and movement there." My father is very attentive to every word I say, as if hearing it for the first time. I continue, my hand now on my eyes, "His eyesight and his short and long term memory were badly affected. At first he was severely handicapped, unable to do anything. But now he is much better."

"Everyday I get better. When I get sick doctors say throw away, no good anymore, but I get better. I no say perfect but not for throw away."

Christos has gotten more than he had bargained for but, seemingly unperturbed, he questions my father "And why are you here today? Are you here to see the doctor?"

My father looks at me to answer.

"Yes, he has an infection under his eye. Nothing serious."

At that point we are called in by the nurse. A quick 'good-bye' leaves the 'old-friend' standing alone.

We enter a small room, lighted by a single bulb, which is made smaller by work benches against three of the four walls. A reading lamp is also on and the room accommodates two chairs. One situated in the centre for the patient, the other near the lamp. A doctor is nowhere to be seen. A nurse is in charge, "Please sit down," she says, pointing to the chair in the middle of the room.

"Sit down, Papa," I instruct 'the old man', who is ill at ease.

"Here?" he asks, while taking slow deliberate steps towards the chair, his hands reaching out in front of him.

"Yes, Papa," I lend a hand, more to remind him that I am here than to help him into the chair.

With my father seated the nurse leaves the room, clipboard in hand. I take the opportunity to inspect the room more closely. My father has no questions. The minutes pass. Outside we hear laughter as nurses share a joke and a tea trolly rattles past, ten to ten on the clock. The nurse returns with a smile and a chair for the 'helpful son'.

"Here you are."

"Thank you."

"Sit down anywhere you like."

The nurse places her clipboard on a bench and faces my father.

Flicking a switch she illuminates an eye chart next to 'the old man'.

"Could you look at the mirror on the wall please ?" she asks, pointing to the wall opposite 'the old man'.

"Hold this and cover your right eye."

She hands my father a piece of cardboard and helps him cover his right eye.

"Look at the mirror, do you see the chart?" she asks, pointing at the chart with her pen.

"Do you see the eye chart, Papa?"

"Yes."

"All right now, tell me which letter I am pointing to."

She points to the letter M on the second line from the top.

No response from 'the old man'.

"Which letter is this Mr Papadopoulos?"

Hesitantly he replies, "Um ..... P!"

"Ah ..... ha ..... all right, now cover your left eye."

She helps him place the cardboard over the left eye.

"Now which letter am I pointing to?"

She points to the letter A on the top line.

"Um ..... I not sure ..... I tell lie ..... I no see perfect. I get sss ....."

"Stroke"

"Stroke. I get stroke, I no see perfect."

The nurse turns to me, "Does your father read English?"

"Yes, he used to, but the stroke affected his eye-sight and his reading ability. I think he can see the letters but cannot interpret them."

"I understand."

Undaunted she replaces the chart with one containing only the letter E facing in different directions.

"We'll try this chart Mr Papadopoulos. Look at the letter E, that I am pointing to and tell me or show me which way 'the legs' are pointing.

She points to the letter E on the second row from the top, which is pointing up.

"Which way is this pointing?"

No response from the 'the old man'.

"Which way is the letter pointing, Papa?"

"This way," says my father, pointing left.

"And this one?" she points to one pointing right.

"Um ..... this way."

Again he points left.

She asks me, "Does he understand what he is supposed to do?"

"I think so. Papa, see the E's on the chart?"

"Yes."

"When the nurse asks you, show her which way the three legs of the E she points to are pointing."

"Oh, I understand."

We are encouraged.

The nurse points to the top line, the biggest E. It is pointing down.

"Which way is this pointing, Mr Papadopoulos?" she asks.

"Um ….. this way."

He points to the left.

"No, Papa!"

"Which way are the legs pointing? The three legs," she pleads.

"I no see perfect. I get sssssstroke. I see letter but I no understand. It get mixed up."

On goes another chart.

"Tell me, Mr Papadopoulos, which animal am I pointing to. Take your time, no need to hurry."

The nurse points to a picture of a horse on the second line.

"What animal is it, Papa? A horse, pig, cat?"

"Um ..... I tell lie ..... um ..... dog."

Final defeat!

"All right, Mr Papadopoulos, that will do for now. Could you wait outside please and the doctor will be with you shortly."

She helps me lead 'the old man' to the waiting bench outside.

"When did he have his stroke?" she asks.

"About two years ago. I think he can see the figures but can't put a meaning to them. I'm sorry."

"That's all right. The eye test is only a formality anyway. If you'll wait here the doctor will see you in a little while."

"Thank you."

*

While waiting and halfway through 'a letter to the editor' my attention is again drawn to Christos Yanapoulos. He appears this time with a lady beside him. She is also dressed in blue hospital attire. She greets my father with uncomplicated affection.

"Vasily! Vasily!"

She hugs and kisses 'the old man'. Warned by her gesturing advance, my father braces himself and accepts her greeting.

"Vasily! How are you?"

'The old man' tries, as usual. "Good, but I no see perfect."

A slight pause and then the blow.

"I no see perfect. Do I know you?"

She steps back and releases one of his hands, it drops slowly to his side.

"Sorry, my father had a stroke a couple of years ago and his memory and eyesight are not very good."

"Oh, I understand."

She looks at 'the old man', "Vasily, it's Poppy Yanapoulos. From South Yarra. Christos and Poppy Yanapoulos."

Christos would have warned her but this is an unavoidable trap.

"Vasily, it's Poppy!," adds Christos.

"Poppy Yanapoulos, from South Yarra," repeats 'the old man'.

A little wait, then he adds, at last, "How are you?"

"Good, and you? How are you friend?"

We explain his situation to them and why he is here today and answer other questions. The atmosphere becomes more relaxed although tainted by their sympathy and 'the old man's' vagueness. I introduce myself as the little boy they once knew and we share a joke about the years.

*

After a little while the reunion is interrupted by a call from the nurse, "Mr Papadopoulos, the doctor will see you now." Before my father and I follow her in to see the doctor we exchange addresses with Christos and Poppy and enthusiastically promise to see each other soon.

We follow the nurse into a different room, much larger than the first. The doctor is there reading some notes on 'the old man'.

"Mr Papadopoulos, how are you?"

"Good. Better."

"Could you sit down here please?"

My father sits facing the doctor.

No seat for 'the helpful son' on this occasion.

"How is your eye today, Mr Papadopoulos?"

"Much better"

"Lets have a look, shall we?"

The doctor swings round some sort of eye inspection machine and adjusts it to my father's height. He then rests my father's chin on the machine and proceeds to give the eye an inspection.

"Please look up, Mr Papadopoulos."

"Look up, Papa."

"Look to the left."

"Left, Papa."

The nurse returns after leaving us with the doctor. She has brought with her what appears to be a group of trainee nurses.

"Right please, Mr Papadopoulos."

"Look right, Papa."

The nurse whispers something to the trainees and points to 'the old man'.

It seems he has gained some notoriety.

"Please look down."

"Look down, Papa."

"Ah, ha. Look up once more, please."

"Look up again, Papa."

I hope the trainees are taking all this in.

"All right, that's fine Mr Papadopoulos."

The doctor jots down some more notes into my Dad's file.

"Has he been applying his eye cream regularly?"

"Yes, three times a day, as you told us."

"I see."

Some more notes.

"His infection looks to have almost cleared. I've written a prescription for two more weeks supply of the eye cream."

He hands me the prescription.

"I think that should see him through."

"Should we continue using it three times a day, as we have been?"

"Yes, for the full two weeks."

With that he hands me the appointment card and the other forms. I then notice my father is still looking up, his chin resting firmly on the machine.

"That's all, Papa, we've finished. Let's go."

We say goodbye to the Doctor and the nurse and leave the room, walking past where the trainee nurses had been moments before.

*

With our prescription filled at the hospital pharmacy, all our adhesive labels used, our appointment card stamped, we leave the hospital for home, avoiding most obstacles.

Part Three:

The inscription on the plaque next to the door reads 'Greek Sub-Branch R.S.L. Victoria.'

"This is it," I say, "come on."

Three figures enter through an open doorway, silhouetted against the fierce afternoon sunlight by the darkness of the corridor within. On the left a tall lean figure moving easily, quickly. In the centre a slightly shorter stouter silhouette, uncertain. On the right, helping to lead the second, a figure shorter and more obese than the other two, veiled and the only woman of the three. My mother, father and I arrive.

Halfway along the corridor, through a lighted doorway, a crowd is viewing the happenings in a room.

We are late for this meeting of the R.S.L. and no one is aware of our arrival. Joining the others at the door I am able to see over the crowd into the room. In front of a crowd, of which we now help constitute the right side, stands a jovial looking chap dressed formally and holding a rolled form in his right hand. On his left another gentleman passes him rolled forms from a table. Both men are wearing war decorations on their chest and are concentrating keenly, although not overly seriously, on their tasks.

The jovial looking chap speaks.

"George Sfikas, Albanian Front 1941."

George steps forward to accept his rolled certificate and a handshake.

"Chris Kostas, Albanian Front 1941."

Chris Kostas does likewise.

Behind the speaker, seated in a row of wooden chairs, are the distinguished members of the R.S.L.

The ceremony continues.

"Arthur Savopoulos, Albanian Front 1941."

An uncurtained window lights the room from behind the seated members.

"Alexis Yanouli, Bulgarian Front 1945."

"Jim Costantinos, Albanian Front 1941."

"John Georges, Albanian Front 1941."

"Angelo Sismanis, Bulgarian Front 1945."

*

Standing next to me, my parents are unable to see over the crowd into the room.

"Paul, what is happening?" asks my mother.

"It looks like they're giving out certificates to men who fought in 'The War'.

"Stephanos Mangos, Albanian Front 1941."

"Ask someone who we have to see to make your father a member."

"Not now, Mama, after the end of the ceremony."

Just in front of my mother a tall moustached man has succeeded, up to now, in ignoring us and to concentrate on the proceedings in the room.

My mother nudges him in the arm, "Excuse me, we have a letter to come here and join. Who should we see about this?"

"Sorry, what did you say?"

"Petros Alexandros, Albanian Front 1941," continues the speaker.

"We have a letter," my mother shows the man the letter, "to come here and join."

"Michael Lengios, Bulgarian Front 1945."

"Can I see the letter?"

The tall moustached man doesn't seem to mind his viewing of the ceremony being interrupted and kindly looks over the letter my mother hands to him.

"Oh yes, you should see the Secretary about this. That's him handing out the certificates. After he has finished, go and see him."

"Who do I have to see?" asks my mother again.

"The Secretary over there, see?"

He steps aside and points out the Secretary to my mother.

"Nick Ellitis, Crete 1943" announces the Secretary.

"Yes, all right, thank you," says my mother.

"What happening?" asks my father.

"They're handing out certificates to those who fought in 'The War', Papa."

"Con Diamond, Albanian Front 1941."

'The old man' pays attention to the goings on for the first time and stretches to peer into the room.

"Who give certificate?" asks my father.

"The Secretary of the R.S.L. Papa."

Another man next to me explains that there is plenty of viewing space at the back of the room and if I were to take 'the old man' there he could see everything.

"Come on, Papa, Mama."

We walk to the end of the corridor and enter through another door, this one leading to the back of the room.

Finding a place where we have a clear view of most of the goings on in the room we stand, quietly, attentively.

"Panayiotis Secoulidis, Crete 1943."

*

"Christos Yamin, Crete 1943."

Christos is a short white haired man with a thick white moustache. He is bespectacled and leaning on a walking stick. He wears a hat and is dressed in an old suit. He tries to hide a slight limp as he walks up to accept his certificate and handshake.

"Jim Raftopoulos, Crete 1943."

Jim is slightly taller and leaner than Christos and has a thick black moustache which completely covers his upper lip. He is dressed in a new suit and his head is bare. He has a full head of jet black hair, combed back and a little greying on the sides. High cheek bones, deep laughter lines and thick black eyebrows frame dark eyes.

"Stylionos Mitropoulos, Albanian Front 1941."

"Nikos Metaxos, Bulgarian Front 1945."

"Arthur Sadaris, Albanian Front 1940."

A woman steps forward veiled and dressed in traditional widow black. She accepts the certificate for deeds now forty years old.

'The old man' has a face that grins widely when amused, frowns sternly when he disapproves and sulks childishly when sad. A face that completely reveals 'the old man's' feelings without him having to say a word. During the ceremony, once 'the old man' knew what was happening, he remained very quiet, totally still and attentive, almost, I imagined, at 'attention'. He stood watching every detail as best he could, jaw firm and serious, his stance upright and his blue eyes a little watery.

*

The final certificate is handed out and the secretary makes a short address thanking those responsible for the success of the meeting. He gives a final compliment to the recipients of the certificates and then the crowd begins to disperse.

"It finished," asks the 'the old man'.

"Yes, Papa."

"Where is the secretary?" asks my mother.

"Over there," I say, pointing to a bald head shining just over the top of the crowd.

Reaching the secretary we find him joking with a couple of certificate recipients and sipping a small cup of hot Greek coffee.

Excusing herself my mother interrupts, explaining who we are and presenting the secretary with the letter we received.

"Oh, yes! Mr Papadopoulos, how are you? I'm glad you could come here today." Says the secretary, by way of a greeting.

"I happy to be here. I am an old soldier. I fight in 'the war.' I wish to join," replies 'the old man'.

"Yes, Mr Papadopoulos, we'll do that in a minute. Have some coffee and there are some cakes over there."

The secretary returns to the conversation he was having with the two veterans. The room has almost emptied, with those remaining talking in little groups, enjoying their coffee and cake.

"Mr Papadopoulos, you say you fought in 'the war'? asks the secretary, finally turning his attention to 'the old man'.

"Yes, from the beginning, when I was a boy, to the end. Against the Italians in Albania and the Germans in The Peloponnese," answers 'the old man'.

He neglects to mention to the secretary of his years as a Partisan Communist fighter during the 'civil war'. Maybe some other time.

"And why do you want to join us now?" I think we first sent you a letter some years ago. It's not for the dances and the outings, is it?"

He asks the question half seriously, posing it as much to my mother as to 'the old man.'

"Because I am an 'old soldier.' I fought for many years and many of my friends die."

A few years earlier when my father was well and the first letter arrived from the R.S.L. 'the old man' said he was too busy to join and that he was not interested in remembering 'the war'.

"I am an old soldier. I fight against the Italians at the start of 'the war' and I still fight until the end."

"Well, Mr Papadopoulos, follow me to the office and we'll get you registered."

The secretary leads us out of the room and up some stairs into a large office. The office has two desks with his desk being on the right, next to a window overlooking the street. In the street, people are still leaving the building. A procession led by running screaming children and followed, a long way behind, by their grandparents – the 'veterans'.

Sunlight through the window casts long shadows into the room. Sitting on chairs near the other desk are some other officials of the R.S.L.

Two are counting raffle tickets, another is reading a Greek newspaper, while another is making some sort of entry into a ledger. On the walls hang pictures of famous war heroes from the past. Long haired bearded or moustached Greeks dressed in the military garb of the Greek Army of the War of Independence. A map of Greece hangs over the secretary's chair and near the centre of the room are pictures of the President of Greece and The Queen of England.

*

The secretary, sitting in his chair with papers covering his desk is a picture of clerical efficiency. Not a word is spoken as he scribbles details onto a form. A few particulars about 'the old man'- name, address, age.

"When and where did you fight?" asks the secretary, as a matter of course.

"Against the Italians in Albania and the Germans in The Peloponnese and later as a guerrilla in 'the resistance'. From the start of 'the war' until the Germans were defeated. For many years I fight. I join as a boy."

The secretary jots down this information.

"Where did you join?"

"In Patra."

"What year?"

"I do not remember. At the start of the war."

"Can you remember any of your personal particulars? Your identification number, any of your regiments' numbers, which officers you fought under?"

"No, I'm sorry. I cannot remember."

"If you could remember some details we could look up your records in Greece and get the information we require from there."

"No, I cannot remember any names or numbers. I'm sorry. I can only remember what happened. I get sss....."

"Stroke. My father suffered a stroke a couple of years ago and parts of his memory were badly affected."

I explain my father's condition to the secretary and why he cannot remember any of the details of his military service during 'the war.'

"I see. I'm sorry but we cannot officially register you as a Returned Serviceman or issue you with a Certificate of Service in 'the war', without some written confirmation from Greece. Can't you remember any details, an officer's name, any name, any number at all?"

"No, I cannot," apologizes 'the old man.'

"Do you have any Medals or Military Decorations or any paperwork that you received during 'the war'?"

"I don't know," my father answers.

"They were lost twenty years ago when we were in South Yarra," my mother explains. "He had an old bag with medals in it."

"Do you know what kind of Medals they were? Can you describe them?" the secretary asks my mother.

"No."

"I'm sorry, the best I can do for you Mr Papadopoulos is to invite you to our functions as a 'guest of the R.S.L.'"

"He fight in war many, many years. He has shrapnel scars and wounds all over his body!" exclaims my mother.

"I fight against the Italians and the Germans and in 'the resistance.' I am an old soldier."

It is of no use, the secretary cannot accept my father for membership or for a certificate without some sort of written proof. We try again but to no avail. The secretary again makes his point and tries to console us with the promise that we will still be invited to all their functions. We leave with only that for consolation.

*

Recently I spoke to 'the old man', the day after an R.S.L. function in which he was given the honour of sitting at the same table as the secretary. We spoke at length about a few things. I asked him if he had a good time at the function the night before and he said he did. I mentioned something about his friends Christos and Poppy Yanapoulos whom we had met a few months earlier at the hospital. I suggested to him that maybe we should go and visit them since it had been a while since seeing them and they hadn't contacted us yet. He said he didn't care and looked away.

Part Four:

A couple of weeks later.

"How are you, Papa?"

"Better ..... everyday better. I don't say I get perfect but I improve. When I get sick, when I get sss....."

"Stroke."

"Stroke. When I get stroke, doctors say throw away, no good any more. But now I am better. I don't say perfect, but not for throw away. And you? Are you good?"

"Yes, Papa, very good."

"What you do today, Paul? You work?"

"No, Papa. Today I and a few friends go to the beach."

"Good, enjoy yourself. You see your girl today Paul?"

"Yes."

"You see her every day?"

"Yes, Papa, every day."

"Good."

He is very pleased for me.

"Papa, I would like to read you a story I write. Would you like to hear it?"

"Yes, come closer, over here."

"Wait, I'll get it."

'The old man' makes himself comfortable in a 'Garden Seat' and I rush and get the manuscript to this story. He has often heard a story or poem from me and given praise or mild criticism in return. I think he is glad to do so.

"This is a story I write, Papa, 'His weight rested easily in the chair. The big man, although appearing awkward, sat relaxed comforted by the early morning winter sun. .....'"

I read my story to him, slowly and clearly, correcting my errors as I go.

"That's it. Did you like it, Papa?"

"Yes, very good Paul. Always keep on writing. Never stop, no matter what anybody say."

"Yes, Papa."

"Never stop writing."

"Yes, Papa. I like writing very much. I find it special. I want to express how I feel, what I think and feel about life, Papa."

"Yes, Paul. You write good. Never stop writing.

I look over what I've written in the light of my revelation to my father and my father's approval. I don't know. What did I say, "express what I think and feel about life?"

"Tell me Paul"

"Yes, Papa."

"In the story did you say anything about God?"

* * * * * * * * * * * * * *

[All Poems and Writings © Peter Stavropoulos 2020]

Thank you for reading my book. If you enjoyed it could you please leave a review.

Best Wishes,

Peter Stavropoulos.

www.ingramcontent.com/pod-product-compliance
Lightning Source LLC
Chambersburg PA
CBHW071313200626
46813CB00015B/2097